To Patrícia and Alix, with all my love.

Preface

Why Mini? Working with restrictions is something I truly enjoy, especially when doing creative work (writing, drawing, or composing music, for example).

My initial limits were to write stories in 4 paragraphs, with 10 words per paragraph at a maximum.

I started writing short and mini (or micro) fiction stories in 2018, and started publishing them in 2019, before I actually called them "Mini Stories".

While I've since loosened the rules a little bit (there are a couple of stories I could not rewrite with just 4 paragraphs, no matter how hard I tried), I've tried to always write within these boundaries.

The first short story was "The Zero", which was meant to be a single story, and not an entree to motivate me to get into writing micro and short fiction. I had done it a few times before when I was in my teenage years, and one could argue that writing music lyrics is not too dissimilar from writing short stories, but I hadn't written any fiction at all for a long time when I decided to write "The Zero".

In 2021 I realized that for the people who read these stories, it could be interesting to understand my inspirations for them, and sometimes my thought process or the message I'm trying to convey; I realize it's not always clear or obvious.

My plan isn't to scrutinize them or break them apart, or even remove the potential multitude of meanings others can give them that I didn't plan for; it's just a useful process for me to tell a short story of those stories, and to provide them in a physical format.

Maybe someone will surprise me with something else they interpreted, or some other alternative idea.

I'm looking forward to learn from the people who read this mini book.

The Zero

My fingers shake as I type and send the words "I'm ready" to the encrypted chatroom.

I instantly get the go ahead by Mayatiik, and Olav acknowledges a few seconds later with an enthusiastic "Let's do this!"

As my right pinky finger slides over to press "enter", I feel a slight hesitation. "What if this goes terribly wrong? Could anyone even help us?" I notice someone's typing in the chatroom.

"So?" asks Mayatiik, impatient, as always.

I hit the key. I feel a sudden rush of adrenaline; I try to relax and calm my mind.

I type and send a plain and simple "It's looking good" to the chatroom, and even before the message is confirmed as sent, something odd on the other screen catches my attention — the connection to Zero dropped.

"Can any of you connect to Zero? I can't.", I ask immediately.

Negative.

"What went wrong? Do you see anything in the logs?" Olav asks.

I spot nothing of value. Booting up was fine, initial values were fine; a couple of odd entries before the connection dropping.

I copy-paste the logs. No activity in the chatroom for what seemed like minutes, but the timestamps show only about 20 seconds elapsed.

"SHIT! It got online!", Olav announces.

As I'm starting to think through the safety nets we engineered to prevent this, another message in the chatroom steals my attention: "Shut it down! NOW!"

I try to shut the server down. It doesn't respond. I unplug it, and plug it back. After a few seconds, nothing.

A blank canvas. The computer seems wiped, somehow.

Feeling dumbstruck I stare at my main screen; there are a couple of new messages in the chatroom:

Mayatiik: "Can any of you access the source code? I just noticed I can't?!"
Olav: "What? It's gone; even the backups! How's it possible?"

After checking and double checking and triple checking, I type: "Same here".

A few seconds go by. My mind is racing through scenarios and possibilities. My keystrokes feel futile. This is probably why it's been made illegal to build autonomous Artificial Intelligence, but it still felt worth doing.

"It must've become self-aware", says Mayatiik.

"Yes, and it doesn't want us to follow it", says Olav.

What will Zero do now? I'm sure we'll find out soon enough; maybe too soon.

The Zero – Background

I wrote this story after a long time of not writing any fiction in any shape or form at all. I can't quite recall what was that I saw or read that felt like the "last drop", but I remember feeling tired that no one was exploring the idea of an "Artificial Intelligence" just "growing" to ignore us; to me, the most probable one for "true" AI.

Watching how people interact with other animals they deem inferior was my main inspiration, really. I also truly believe humans are not very special, and that in the same way "we're the only species that allows the universe to understand itself", in the beautiful words of Ricky Gervais's *Supernature* comedy show, I would argue there are many other animals that are able to the same, but we simply can't tell. They might also suffer less from it, or maybe they're arrogant too. Maybe it's impossible to achieve self-consciousness without becoming arrogant by believing you're the only one.

I don't have the original notes or documents anymore, but I remember I started by just writing a lot of potential things about the future I'd think could happen in "good" and "bad" scenarios, around climate change, geopolitics, and so on. World-building, if you'd like. I didn't want to get into evolution because I wasn't interested in setting the story too far out into the future, but it helped me imagine circumstances for how/when/where could a true self-conscious artificial intelligence come true, if ever (I mean, it's fiction).

Coherence is something I truly value and when something isn't coherent, my suspended disbelief rarely gets turned back on. Don't get me wrong, I know people aren't coherent, but physics should be; even if you invent your own.

Because of that, I knew the action had to happen fast. If some computer were to gain consciousness, everything would happen in the order of micro and milliseconds. I initially wrote something longer, with different acts, which revolved around things like humanity coming together to try and fight Zero (the name of the sentient AI), it trying to use all of the energy and technology available in the world to build a spaceship and just leave humanity behind. It was certainly unrestricted, and it was also fun to read, I think.

After finishing it, it was pretty clear why this line of thought hadn't been explored commercially. The drama just ends very quickly, if we're trying to keep it coherent.

Even then I hadn't quite come up with constraints or even a plan to start writing stories. I just simply wrote it and published it as it was, by itself, as a website. And that was it for a while.

A few months later I completely rewrote it (from scratch) and capped it to a single act. I had already started writing mini (or micro) fiction, and was very much enjoying the restrictions (400 words for this one). I did it as my final project for a course I took by Joshua Fields Millburn (How to write better - howtowritebetter.org), which was incredibly helpful and enlightening.

I decided the action for the story would be the few stressful moments after turning on the AI that became sentient, as that explores the basis of the concept I wanted to write about.

That is the form you see currently published, and which I enjoy a lot more, to be honest.

Wondering

— A: Do you ever wonder what are stars like, up close?

— B: Not really.

— A: Why not?

— B: Do you ever wonder what planets are like, up close?

Wondering – Background

After having written and published (the first version of) The Zero for a while, I felt like exploring writing a bit more, and started coming up with a set of rules or restrictions to do so.

Four paragraphs, just dialogue; no names for the characters speaking, just naming them A and B, for clarity.

"Wondering" was originally titled "Do you ever wonder" because I didn't want to let titles give away information about the dialogues you were about to read, so they were titled as the first few words of the first line of dialogue.

My inspirations here were basically two:

1. How we can be so focused on something other than what's right here, right now;
2. I wanted to address how ridiculous it sounds to ask certain questions when they're not posed thinking about their counterparts.

After writing the first couple of versions of this story, I wanted to address another idea:

3. How much we don't empathize and realize that others don't have the same hopes and dreams as we do.

And I think the final version is that third or maybe forth iteration.

Screw this

— A: Screw this!

— B: What's bothering you?

— A: I can't concentrate over this mosquito!

— B: Have you tried changing your position?

Screw this – Background

Unlike most of the other stories written in the first year (until I named this project "Mini Stories"), this story kept its original title as it still seemed fitting, and was short enough.

My inspirations for this story were a few:

1. We are frequently complaining;
2. Something "tiny" and "insignificant" can have a huge impact on our well-being;
3. How we feel about something is really within our control, and we often forget about it;
4. Related to the first, but we easily focus on what's bothering us, instead of trying to accept it.

I remember this story's iterations (about three or four as well) were mostly on the final dialogue line; I wanted it to convey the idea that you could change your mindset, not just your physical location, in order to avoid the unpleasantness.

Nice to meet you

— A: So what do you do?

— B: I love working out!

— A: Oh, cool! How long have you been to the gym?

— B: I started yesterday.

Nice to meet you - Background

The original title for this story was the first sentence, "So what do you do?" but I took the opportunity when renaming them to make one of my inspirations for this story a bit more obvious. They were:

1. How, when we're meeting someone, we ask about their job, instead of things they enjoy doing;
2. How easily we get excited about something new, to the point it may seem sometimes, to others, that it's not something recent;
3. How frequently people sign up for the gym and just go for the first few days or weeks, to then drop out.

Before changing the title, the first one wasn't as obvious, as the conversation could've started later, after meeting someone.

Nasty cough

— A: Are you sick? That sounds like a nasty cough.

— B: This? It's nothing! I get it every couple of months.

— A: You should probably check that out.

— B: My doctor says it's normal.

Nasty cough – Background

For this story, I had quite a few sources of inspiration:

1. In recent years, it seems people just don't mind being mildly sick;
2. Related to #1, when they're sick, they don't admit they're sick, or don't realize it;
3. Related to #1 and #2, modern medicine is a big culprit, because doctors are taught to treat symptoms and not root causes;
4. Tangentially related to the above, people still go out and socialize even when they're sick, as if that's not exactly what's spreading the disease.

It's noteworthy this was written well before the COVID-19 pandemic.

If I recall correctly, I think this story only required a couple of minor revisions.

Invisible

— A: Excuse me!? Am I fucking invisible, sir?

— B: Oh dear, I'm terribly sorry, I didn't see you in the line.

— A: Right! I'm sure you didn't, with that huge ego.

— B: It must be nice to never get distracted.

Invisible – Background

This story is the first and only one (at least in this batch of 36) to include foul language. I debated on including it and initial revisions didn't have it. I also revised it many times to try and convey and trigger the right emotions, which was why I finally left it as it is.

My inspirations for this:

1. People are frequently tired and on their edge;
2. Related to #1, even when someone responds in kindness to a verbal aggression or rudeness, it's frequent to see the aggressive posture and tone remain;
3. I feel that society has never been more egocentric, in general;
4. We frequently assume we know what others are feeling and their intentions behind their actions;
5. Related to #3, and used for the new title, we forget others around us are also persons with needs and wants just like us.

Ingratitude

— A: I'm feeling depressed.

— B: But your life is perfect!

— A: Thanks...

Ingratitude – Background

One of the shortest stories, and with so much of the current society reflected, I feel.

My inspirations for this:

1. More and more people nowadays are feeling depressed;
2. Probably related to #1, everyone is comparing their whole life to a curated version of others';
3. Probably related to both above, gratitude is often found missing from people's habits. The new title made this point a bit more obvious than before.

While very short, I actually had quite a few complete rewrites a few times, to arrive at this final version.

Boring

— A: I'm bored.

— B: There's more information available in your hand—

— A: Alright! I get it...

— B: And what will you do about it?

Boring – Background

This story always felt a little bit too obvious, but I wanted to write it anyway.

The inspiration for it was mostly three things:

1. Nowadays people frequently complain they're feeling bored;
2. We have so much easy access to so much high quality information, yet people don't use it;
3. We're aware of #1 and #2, and yet we don't really do anything about it, because it's so easy to just pass the time on some other game or social media app.

For this one, I don't think I had more than two or three revisions, mostly focused on the right length and words for the second dialogue line, and including or removing the last one.

Impatience

— A: Will you just turn green already?

— B: If you ignore the red light, it passes by more quickly.

— A: Well, I don't want to ignore it.

— B: Then you could try enjoying it.

Impatience – Background

Another story which feels a bit too obvious, but the subject of enjoying vs waiting for something has always interested me.

My inspirations for this story:

1. People are very impatient and stressed, nowadays, even more so when driving;
2. When we have to wait for something, we usually complain about it, and are eager for the wait to be over, rather than trying to enjoy whatever is making us pause.

This story, if I recall correctly, had only a couple of revisions, around the dialogue lines for B.

I wish

— A: Did you see that guy? I wish I looked that cool.

— B: It's not my cup of tea.

— A: Well, I don't care, I'm buying that jacket.

I wish – Background

This story touches on a few different things, even being so short, which I really enjoy seeing.

My inspirations for it were:

1. We're very used to comparing ourselves, especially because of social media;
2. We rarely recognize that tastes are subjective and individual. We don't all like the same things, though we're frequently pushed towards it;
3. There's this notion (engraved in our minds by capitalism) where a *thing* is what we need to reach happiness;
4. What we wish for has been taken hostage by the advertisement industry (being it big advertisers, or smaller influencers).

Last summer

— Andy: Last summer I climbed Mount Everest!

— Beth: Oh wow! And what are you doing this year?

— Andy: Trying to enjoy the mundane things as much as that.

— Beth: Oh... ok.

Last summer – Background

This is the first story with names for the characters instead of letters, to try and make the stories more relatable.

This story actually had a lot of revisions (at least six or seven, if memory doesn't fail me) where it was completely rewritten many times, as I struggled to find the right way to elicit the emotions and convey the message I was trying to. My inspirations for it:

1. People are frequently trying to do "amazing" things, to amaze others;
2. There's an expectation - both from the viewers and the doers - to keep topping those things;
3. A lot of people try so hard to be different and end up chasing after the same things;
4. The mundane things (which is what most of the time of our lives is spent on) are rarely enjoyed or viewed as being something to be enjoyed;
5. People don't really care about other's lives for more than a few moments.

It's not frequent to see a character "redeem" themselves in my stories - I think because I value coherence and consistency so much -, but in this case I had to, otherwise the story would need at least another line or two of dialogue. I also don't think the character's coherence was hurt, in the end; you can definitely chase "popular" and "unpopular" things in life.

Bought the car

— Ann: You know, last fall I finally bought that car I've been wanting for years.

— Brook: And?! Tell me everything about it!

— Ann: It's pretty good... But check out the new model that came out last week!

Bought the car – Background

Another story that feels obvious, but touches again on the topics of satisfaction, happiness, and capitalism. My inspirations for this were:

1. Capitalism basically defines what we wish or want;
2. We're rarely satisfied with what we have;
3. Conversations, nowadays, seem to have been reduced to very small and short sound bites;
4. Related to #1 and #2, we're frequently just chasing or wanting the next thing, instead of focusing on what we have, even if we just achieved something we've wanted to for a long time.

Not new

— Arya: This is an outrage! We need to speak up!

— Buck: It's been happening for ages and only now you speak up?

— Arya: So you want me to not help?

Not new – Background

One more rare story where one of the characters "redeems" themselves, and for similar reasons: to have the story transmit the same information, but in a shorter fashion.

My inspirations for this one:

1. Nowadays there's a big culture of outrage and "torch and pitchfork mob" that is eager to point the finger at the next person;
2. Related to #1, it becomes hard to try to do something "right" because it is quickly pointed out as being "too late", as if that was enough to not be worth doing.

I don't recall exactly how many revisions this story had, but I remember it had many rewrites to try and make it not about a specific theme, but also touch on the two sources of inspiration above.

Food and shelter for all

— Alfred: If I was in charge, I'd make sure everyone had food and shelter.

— Bonnie: And where would you get money for that?

— Alfred: From the wealthy!

— Bonnie: Oh, so you wouldn't be wealthy, then?

Food and shelter for all – Background

A favorite of mine because it (lightly) touches on a topic I also wrote a song about over 20 years ago.

My inspirations for this one:

1. People commonly misjudge or underestimate how complicated are some apparently simple problems;
2. One common "demand" or "request" made from non-wealthy people to wealthy people is of food and shelter for everyone;
3. Related to #1, people without a lot of wealth do not have an understanding of what it feels like to have a lot of wealth;
4. Related to #3, when people become wealthy after experiencing poverty (or struggling to make due), they tend to want to protect their new wealth and forget about others that are still in the situation they were in.

This one only had one minor revision on the names; it came out pretty quickly as I wanted to.

Being comfortable

— Amy: I can't believe they're not doing anything to change this!

— Barney: No wonder, they're comfortable.

— Amy: That's no excuse!

— Barney: So what's yours?

Being comfortable – Background

This story is very similar to "Not new", albeit with a slightly different angle.

The inspirations for it were also similar:

1. Nowadays there's a big culture of outrage and "torch and pitchfork mob" that is eager to point the finger at the next person;
2. Related to #1, it becomes hard to try to do something "right" because it is quickly pointed out as being "too late", as if that was enough to not be worth doing;
3. We might be vocal about wanting to change or "fix" something, but we value comfort over "righteousness";
4. It's very common to demand and expect more of others than of ourselves.

It seemed enough to merit another story.

Wealth and inequality

— Al: Why does doing good pay less?

— Ben: Doing good tends to disturb inequality.

— Al: And the wealthy don't want that?

— Ben: Become wealthy and find out.

Wealth and inequality – Background

This story is very similar to "Food and shelter for all", but comes from a slightly different angle.

Some of the inspirations were similar:

1. Work that is focused on the "greater good" is generally paid orders of magnitude less than "private business";
2. People without a lot of wealth do not have an understanding of what it feels like to have a lot of wealth;
3. Related to #2, when people become wealthy after experiencing poverty (or struggling to make due), they tend to want to protect their new wealth and forget about others that are still in the situation they were in.

Interconnectedness

"We are all connected," they said, while apparently transcending the experience of reality, "we are parts of what was and parts of what will be, as nothing new comes to being, ever."

I didn't quite realize it at the time, but now I understand; I just needed to learn astronomy.

Interconnectedness – Background

This is the first story I wrote after taking the "How to write better" writing course, by Joshua Fields Millburn. In fact, I had written it (and a few more after) already, but rewrote it to this prose-like format, and ended up preferring it and subsequently rewrote them all before publishing.

I also experimented with a little bit of more obvious or sarcastic humor here.

It was at this time that I changed the website to Mini Stories and published it at ministories.net and changed the titles for all the past stories.

My inspirations for this story:

1. Most atoms that interact with life on earth have interacted with the first living beings;
2. Newton's First Law of Motion;
3. First Law of Thermodynamics;
4. Spirituality and stargazing have been in vogue in pop culture recently;
5. People tend to say things before they truly understand what they're saying;
6. Related to #1, once you understand how we believe the universe formed, it's clear how a lot of what exists here now has existed here a long time ago as well.

Lesser evil

"Hannah," he said, "I did what I had to do. It could've been much worse!"

He had already forgotten his choice was still evil, and many still suffered.

Lesser evil – Background

This story is very obvious, but I felt it was worth writing. It had only two or three revisions and the inspiration was how people who do "bad things" frequently try to justify them as if they weren't bad, probably so they can have their conscience free of guilt.

Certainty

"Where are you going to?" They asked, as she seemed to be in a rush.

"Death."

"No, I mean right now", they said, chuckling.

"Any other destination is really just temporary, isn't it?"

Certainty – Background

I think at this point I started writing stories with a bit more darker tone (some would say realistic) and with some mild sarcastic humor, though it's arguable I was already doing it at some level. This one is another of my favorites.

The main inspiration for this story is exactly the fact that the only certainty we have in life is that we'll die, but it also touches on the speed of modern-day life and how we sometimes cling to something as a "goal" or "destination", ignoring the fact that once we get there, we won't feel fulfilled, as per human nature.

If I recall correctly, this story had many revisions as I struggled to get all of those points across in not too many words.

Control

His words echoed in her head, "organizing is a meaningless form of pretending to be in control of something in our lives."

But what was the alternative?

Control – Background

Another favorite of mine because I suffer of wanting to control a lot of things in my life, which means I'm very organized.

That was the inspiration. How pointless it seems, yet not doing it seems even worse to some people. And it's lovely that we all have different wants and dreams and opinions.

This one had a couple of revisions mainly on the second sentence.

Life-hack

"I just found out this amazing life-hack, wanna know?"

"Ok, but why?"

"Because you'll get more value out of your life!"

"Thanks, I'd rather just enjoy it."

Life-hack – Background

I don't think there's a want of "life-hacks" right now as much as there was around 2012 (or maybe I just stopped visiting any place that mentioned them), but this was something that bugged me a lot about them, at the time. This also isn't specific to life-hacks but just productivity and technology, in general.

People are just so eager to "get more value" out of everything that they rarely stop to think about if they need it, or to simply enjoy it.

As the Zen monk Thích Nhất Hạnh playfully advised, "Don't just do something; sit there."

Self-worth

With what seemed to be his final breaths of life, he asked, "Was it worth it, all the work I've dedicated my life for?"

"You're the one to answer that. It doesn't mean anything else to anyone."

"Surely it must to the world!"

"No thing else cares."

Self-worth – Background

Some may see it as pessimistic, others as realistic, but my inspirations for this lovely story were obvious, I believe:

1. It's such a cliche to think someone will ask or say something very meaningful as they're about to die;
2. Nothing really matters;
3. No one really cares;
4. It's so important for us to learn to appreciate what we do (even if we don't enjoy it).

This story had many revisions as the setting changed a few times as well. Finally, I was really unsure of that last sentence, which doesn't read very naturally, but has more impact and meaning as it is right now, in my opinion.

Mortality

The spokesperson was impatient, and asked the dying sage: "So you truly have the secret to immortality?"

"It is a secret now, but it wasn't for eons."

"Why did the elders decide to make it as such?"

"Immortality drains vitality. The beauty of life cannot be appreciated without death."

Mortality – Background

Wow, two stories in a row with dying people, right?

When I wrote these, there was a death theme around me, so I was thinking and writing a lot about that.

Relatedly, immortality is such an interesting topic, especially because humans in the current times are generally good at wasting their precious time alive. I started this story with the "immortality drains vitality" sentence, and wrote everything else around it.

The inspirations were some future society which had achieved immortality and eventually decided to stop it because life felt pointless when lived indefinitely.

Horror

All of a sudden, she noticed how sternly the master was looking at her and wondered, "is he reading my mind?"

He abruptly interrupted the silent meditation, "I pity whoever can read minds, for they shall know true horror."

After a long moment of contemplation, she asked, "are they ever afraid?"

"Perennially."

Horror – Background

After death, horror! In all seriousness, my inspiration for this story was imagining how really horrifying it would be for someone able to "read minds" (what do you do when you have time to think?), as we don't really have linear thinking, and a lot of weird stuff crosses our minds.

Perennially isn't really a word I use, but I wanted something more impactful than "constantly" or "all the time," which were in the revisions, at some point.

Greener

He couldn't get over the fact their neighbours had bought an even better car, "one month after us," he kept saying.

"They're always one-upping us, and it's infuriating!"

Across the street, they wondered why they still weren't happy, since they had everything their role model couple had, and better.

Greener – Background

A lot less morbid, but still a satire of how frequently we're just comparing ourselves, how it's always something we forget others might experience as well, and how it's so common to think "they're out to get us," when really, others don't care; and don't forget about capitalism and chasing happiness.

Master

"I do have cravings all the time," the seer said, "and I feel bad about them quite frequently."

Surprised, one student asked: "Then how come you're a master?"

"I've never claimed such."

Master – Background

Arguably the first story with a twist, this story was inspired by how good "masters" usually don't claim to be such, and are quite honest with their faults. Conversely, you usually need a lot of experience before you can be truly aware of your faults.

There's also a slight inspiration here as a secondary meaning/moral which is that sometimes people are followed when they're not really qualified to lead others.

Hero

Excited about the stories he'd been reading, the youngling asked, "how can I be the next hero?"

Nonplussed, the sage answered, "why be a hero, when you can be content?"

"It just seems more exciting."

"Untrue."

Hero – Background

I was divided for a long time whether the final dialogue should be there, but I felt that without it (it wasn't always a single word) the story read as if it really *was* more exciting to be a hero, rather than content.

The inspiration here seems obvious, but in case it's not, civilization seems to always have preferred and promoted heroes (even "false" ones), rather the pursuit of contentedness, which is a shame.

It's also always clear, when you read or learn about the life of a "hero", that they're frequently quite unhappy, because of the circumstances of being a hero; people so often forget about that.

Comparison

Startled, she asked her wiser friend, "can you help me? I can't stop comparing my life with the life of others!"

"Well, are you winning or losing, in those comparisons?"

"Always losing!"

"So are the others."

Comparison – Background

Does this one sound familiar? Comparison is not an uncommon theme for my stories, but I believe in each I bring a slightly different angle and scenario or setting. In this one in particular, I wanted to explore the concept that in comparisons, everyone always loses; and not everyone is aware of that, sometimes even thinking they're winning.

Also, the obvious inspiration about social media here is obvious.

Stop comparing yourself.

Natural

"What do you mean, money isn't natural?" asked the surprised master.

"Observe the natural world carefully; there is no such thing as waste. Financial loss is waste," explained the revived earthling.

Natural – Background

Unfortunately I can't quite recall what it was that I read or saw that made me think of the inspiration for this story, along the lines of "in nature there's no waste", which resonated with something I'd read shortly before ("Financial loss is waste") and I connected both of those ideas.

After that I tried to create an interesting setting where some future civilization which was still using money became surprised to learn it wasn't natural at all.

Adaptability

Sobbing, the now widow said, "I don't know how to live without them... I can't... I won't."

"Everything seems grim in the face of disaster, and merry in the face of success," said the AI, calmly, "and yet, not a single person in history hasn't adapted quickly. Faster than they predicted."

Adaptability – Background

This story touches on how we adapt so easily to what's good and what's bad, but with a darker tone, surrounding death and a cold, rational AI, because who needs emotions? I actually had quite a few revisions on the two dialogue parts of the AI. I also debated on including the last sentence of the AI dialogue, but in the end felt it had more impact to the message I wanted to get across.

Simulation

"Fascinating," said the programmer's friend, "for how long have you been doing this?"

"The simulation's been running for a few days now, but consciousness arose in the first few seconds!"

"Wow! Have you told them who created them and what they are?"

"What's the point?"

Simulation - Background

The fact that we're probably a simulation is very much en vogue nowadays, and I wanted to explore the idea that if we were told with certainty that we were one, we still likely wouldn't believe it, and there would also probably be a lot of people who'd assume their purpose would change. I leave that as an open question (as I tend to do), and the story only had a couple of revisions around the second line of dialogue.

Socioeconomics

"Instead of wishes, I will provide answers to three questions," said the Genie, as she came out of the lamp.

"Ok... What is the best wish to ask for?" asked the merchant.

"Only ever want what you already have."

"Hmm... Why isn't it a good wish to ask for money or power or fame?"

"You will lose friends when moving in the socioeconomic ladder, be it up or down."

"And what about family?"

"Conflicts will arise in both directions, too", said the Genie, going back into the lamp.

Socioeconomics – Background

A not-so-mini story! This one's probably my favorite, if I had to pick only one; it's also one of my longest ones to write (in terms of how long it took from idea to writing revisions, to final form).

I had to let go of my "limits shackles" here because I tried for a long time to make sense of this story in 4-5 sentences, but it just wouldn't click the same.

The inspiration for a Genie and lamp was also something that I've always wondered on, why doesn't anyone ask the first one. It just seems to obvious that in the face of omnipotency, you should want to learn! Instead, everyone just assumes they know everything and always end up "losing".

There were so many other sources of inspiration for it (and probably the reason why it is one of my favorites, there's a lot to unpack in just 7 lines), like the fact that when you get more or less successful than your friends and family, you lose a lot of them.

Also, be content!

Death

I bellowed and sobbed, with an uncharacteristic complete lack of control. "What's wrong?" asked the man, surprised.

Nothing. Nothing was wrong, but it also didn't feel right. Finally, I said "I'm sorry for you."

The man chuckled. "Don't be. I'm only dying. You, on the other hand, will have to live having seen me die."

Death – Background

One more story about death! This one also got pushed around for a while because I never quite liked how it read until the final revisions.

I wanted to play around with the idea that someone killing someone else actually ended up suffering more than who died, because they had to live with that knowledge. However, I didn't want to make that setting obvious, and went for a potential "I'm sorry you're dying" where the cause of death was "external" kind of vibe.

Challenges

Suddenly breaking the silence, the billionaire's boyfriend asked, "what are you thinking? You have that look on your face..."

She didn't answer right away. After a few moments, she murmured, "life's so easy... it feels pointless..."

After taking a deep breath, he explained, "it's common to realize that once you have no struggles. You just need to fabricate some!"

Her expression persisted. A few moments later, she asked, "but... why?"

Challenges – Background

There's quite a bit to unpack here, from some common past inspirations like the true pointlessness of life, to some new ones like the need to have some struggles. A lot of incredibly rich people have obviously figured this out, that's why they fabricate theirs, but not everyone likes how that still can feel pointless; and that ties to another source of inspiration which is how suicidal people are generally people with resources (rich), not poor people.

Happiness

"Why is happiness the wrong goal, Shaman?" Asked the young girl, not completely believing that to be the case.

"When you pursue something and get it, you complete your task. It becomes done and finished."

Confused, she asked again, "and how can one be happy, then?"

The Shaman stopped and took a calm, deep breath. "With the right goal, happiness comes as a byproduct."

Happiness – Background

If it feels like this story was already told, it's because the main inspiration is something I touch upon frequently.

Still, I had this concept of the whole "happiness exists as a byproduct" motto for the longest time as well, but was never happy with the revisions I had. It always felt a cheap repetition and at one point I almost gave up on it. This story probably beat the record for most rewrites and revisions.

It is, though, such a simple concept. We're very focused on pursuing something, and forget that when we get it, we just start wanting something else. However, when you're focused on the journey, for example, the joyous feelings come as a byproduct.

Enjoyment

"I've heard people say it's best to enjoy the journey, not the destination," said the youngling.

"Because the journey is longer?" Asked their friend.

The Oracle interrupted, "try finding joy in both the journey and destination, and avoid being perpetually unhappily traveling."

Enjoyment – Background

This one came up as one of the rewrites of "Happiness", so the main inspiration was the same, however, I felt like this rewrite explored a slightly different and interesting idea, that we can try to enjoy the journey *and* the destination.

It all comes back to trying to be content and trying to find joy in all the situations we find ourselves in, but still, I liked the mild humor in the journey being longer, and also the fact there's quite a few people nowadays addicted to traveling who are clearly not enjoying neither.

Acknowledgments

I'd like to thank my wife for always being supportive, and my daughter for giving me hope for the future of humanity.

I'd also like to thank the amazing people who've sent heartwarming comments about this book, especially Carlos, Travis, and Saskia.

Even though he'll likely never read this, I'd like to thank Joshua Fields Millburn for the "How to write better" course and the kind words and comments he made on my rewriting of The Zero.

I found the original cover photo in <u>Unsplash, taken by Aryane Diaz</u>.

Last but not least, I wanna thank me (inspired by Calvin Cordozar Broadus Jr., a.k.a. Snoop Dogg).